For all the children who are in the same situation as Zoe, Ana or Victor.

Pilar Serrano

For Natis.

Canizales

ÉGALITᴲ

Today You Can't Play
Egalité Series

© Text: Pilar Serrano, 2018
© Illustrations: Canizales, 2018
© Edition: NubeOcho, 2019
www.nubeocho.com · hello@nubeocho.com

Original title: *Hoy no juegas*
Text editing: Eva Burke and Rebecca Packard
Translation: Claire Storey and Ben Dawlatly

First edition: 2019
ISBN: 978-84-17123-46-8

The publication of this book has been made possible
through the support of The Government of the
Balearic Islands and the Institut d'Estudis Baleàrics.

G CONSELLERIA
O CULTURA,
I PARTICIPACIÓ
B I ESPORTS

institut d'estudis
baleàrics

Printed in China by Asia Pacific Offset,
respecting international labor standards.

VALUES,
FUN &
DIVERSITY

TODAY YOU CAN'T PLAY

Pilar Serrano   Canizales

nubeOCHO

Ana was nervous. Her palms were sweating and she had a tummyache.

Ever since the new girl, Emma, had arrived in her class, everything had turned into one big nightmare.

Recently, Ana hadn't been able to play with her friends Zoe and Victor at recess.

Emma decided what they would play and who could join in.

Before, recess used to be the best part of the day, but now it was a race to see who could make it into "Emma's Club."

One day, Emma told Ana to hand over her sandwich.

Ana knew that if she didn't, Emma wouldn't let her anywhere near the group.

So, despite the fact that it was her favorite ham sandwich and her stomach was growling like a lion, she gave it to Emma.

Ana turned as red as a tomato. She was dying to tape up Emma's mouth to stop her from saying such things.

But she didn't dare shout out in class that Emma was a liar.

And she didn't want to tell her teacher because she was scared everyone would call her a tattletale.

The next morning,
Ana was sick again.

Class had only just begun when a piece of paper started being passed around from table to table. The kids were giggling under their breath.

YESTERDAY ANA WAS KISSING VICTOR IN THE CAFETERIA

Zoe didn't find the note funny at all. She and Victor and Ana had known each other since they were three years old, and they were really good friends. But since Emma had arrived, there had been nothing but problems.

Zoe tore the note up into little pieces.

Victor, are you going to play with your little friends too, or are you coming to play with **everyone else?**

Just so you know, the other day I heard them saying you play soccer like a dizzy duck.

Ana and Zoe shook their heads to deny it. But not knowing who to believe, Victor walked away, following Emma to go and join the other children.

Oh, it's *really* tasty. But I don't plan on giving you any.

Everyone was impressed with the way Zoe faced up to Emma.

At the end of the day, Victor was walking over to his friends Ana and Zoe when Emma caught up with him.

Going off with your girlfriend, Victor?

Maybe tomorrow **you won't be able to play with us...**

During the rest of that week, things started to change. Every day, another child joined them on the bench at recess.

They started suggesting their own games. There were no bosses or clubs, but instead they decided all together what they wanted to do.

Days went by and the "Bench Bunch" grew bigger and bigger. And Emma was getting lonelier and lonelier.

Until one Friday, while everyone was having fun together, they heard a voice asking:

"Can I play?"

Emma looked sad. Was it possible that she had
realized why she was alone?

Perhaps someday, if she decided to change,
she could play with everyone else too.